Beaver: **Amik**

(a-MIK)

Rose hips: **Oginiig**

(o-gi-NEEG)

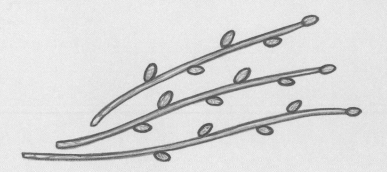

FINDING
MOOSE

by Sue Farrell Holler

Illustrated by
Jennifer Faria

pajamapress

First published in Canada and the United States in 2022

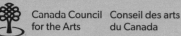 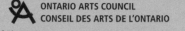 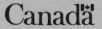

Canada Council for the Arts · Conseil des arts du Canada

ONTARIO ARTS COUNCIL
CONSEIL DES ARTS DE L'ONTARIO
an Ontario government agency
un organisme du gouvernement de l'Ontario

Canada

The publisher gratefully acknowledges the support of the Canada Council for the Arts and the Ontario Arts Council for its publishing program. We acknowledge the financial support of the Government of Canada through the Canada Book Fund (CBF) for our publishing activities.

Library and Archives Canada Cataloguing in Publication

Title: Finding moose / by Sue Farrell Holler ; illustrated by Jennifer Faria.
Names: Holler, Sue Farrell, author. | Faria, Jennifer, illustrator.
Identifiers: Canadiana 20210303220 | ISBN 9781772782448 (hardcover)
Classification: LCC PS8615.O437 F56 2022 | DDC jC813/.6—dc23

Publisher Cataloging-in-Publication Data (U.S.)

Names: Holler, Sue Farrell, author. | Faria, Jennifer, illustrator.
Title: Finding Moose / by Sue Farrell Holler, illustrated by Jennifer Faria.

Description: Toronto, Ontario Canada : Pajama Press, 2022. | Summary: "A little boy goes for a walk in the forest with his grandfather, searching for a moose. The grandfather teaches him to identify the traces left behind by the moose. He also teaches him about other animals and plants found in the forest including the Ojibwemowin names for them. After accepting that their expedition will not be successful that day, the boy and his grandfather return home, only to find the moose grazing behind their house"— Provided by publisher.

Identifiers: ISBN 978-1-77278-244-8 (hardback)

Subjects: LCSH: Grandfathers -- Juvenile fiction. | Moose -- Juvenile fiction. | Animal tracks and signs - Juvenile fiction. | Ojibwa language - Juvenile fiction.| BISAC: JUVENILE FICTION / Family / Multigenerational. | JUVENILE FICTION / People & Places / Canada / Indigenous. | JUVENILE FICTION / Science & Nature / Environment

Classification: LCC PZ7.H655Ra |DDC [E] - dc23

Ojibwemowin translations and pronunciations provided by Janice Simcoe, a member of the Chippewas of Rama First Nation

Original art created with acrylic paint on illustration board
Cover and book design—Lorena González Guillén

Manufactured by Friesens
Printed in Canada

Pajama Press Inc.
11 Davies Avenue, Suite 103 Toronto, Ontario Canada, M4M 2A9

Distributed in Canada by UTP Distribution
5201 Dufferin Street Toronto, Ontario Canada, M3H 5T8

Distributed in the U.S. by Ingram Publisher Services
1 Ingram Blvd. La Vergne, TN 37086, USA

We must be
quiet, quiet
when we go
into the woods.

Soft footsteps and
gentle voices.
Quiet as mice and
rabbits and deer.

"Shhh," I say.

Tired grass crunches on the skinny path.

Ice on the puddle snaps when I step on it.
My boot splashes into water so cold
it makes me dance.

Grandpa taps the ice
with his toe
and lifts a piece,
smooth like a window.

The path goes down past empty trees.
A bird calls **chick-a-dee-dee-dee.**

"All trails lead to water," says Grandpa.
"All animals need to drink."

My tongue hangs out and I slurp like a cat.

We stop when Grandpa sees poop on the trail. It is shiny-brown and shaped like little eggs.

"Moose," he says. "Mooz."

I spread my hands
wide beside my head.
Boy moose have
big antlers.

Grandpa's knees crack like the ice.
He uses a leaf to break open
a moose poop. Inside looks like
chewed-up grass and twigs.

"Fresh," he says.
"Mooz is nearby."

We look all over
for moose prints.

All we find
are boy prints.
And Grandpa prints.

I find tiny purple flowers
hiding in old grass.

And snow that looks like beads
but drips water when I hold it.

Grandpa dries my hands
with the edge of his shirt.
He shows me the branches
where the moose ate breakfast.

Moose is the best at playing
hide and seek. We can't see
him anywhere.

A chipmunk with a
standing-up tail runs
over my boot and
under a broken tree.

Someone hammers fast on wood.
A goose in the sky honks loud.

"Shhh," I say. "We want moose."

I sit beside Grandpa to watch
the creek. The water is slow
at the edge. In the middle,
it bubbles in a circle.

Grandpa takes an apple from
his pocket and cuts it.

I throw a stick into the creek.
It floats and twirls. I get more sticks
and bits of wood. We take turns throwing.

"This one is a gift from **Beaver**," says Grandpa. "**Amik**. See his teeth marks?"

Beaver's teeth make the wood look like ripple chips.

I bite my apple piece and show Grandpa the shape my teeth make.

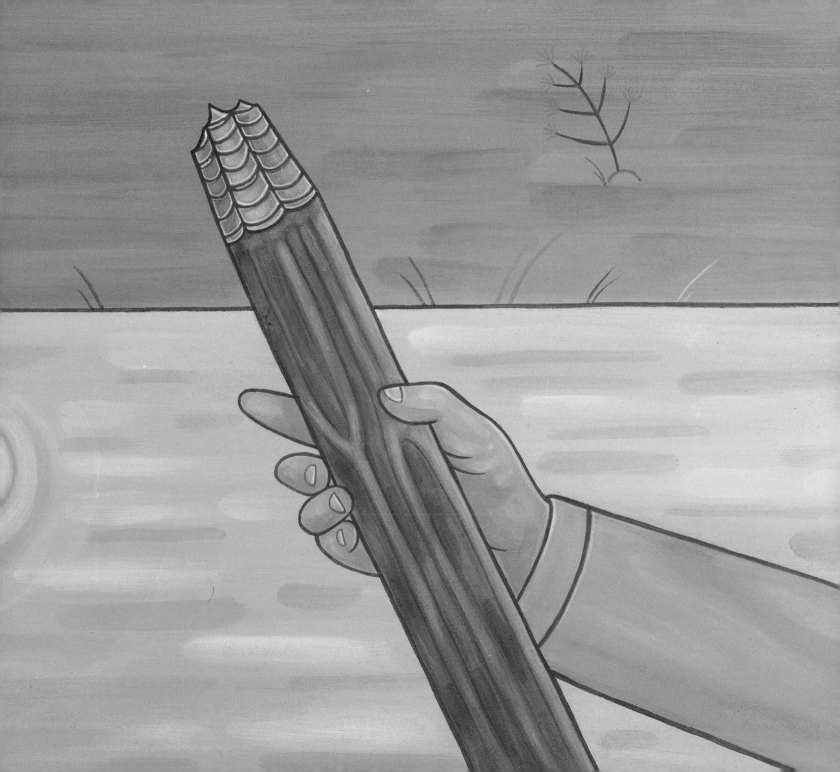

On the way home, Grandpa finds
hairy twigs with red berries.
The berries are fat and round
and wear itsy-bitsy crowns.

"**Rose hips**," he says. "**Oginiig**.
Good for tea."

I help him pick—careful, careful not
to get prickles—until his pocket is full.

Grandpa cuts branches with ends as soft and gray as kittens.

Pussy willows," he says. "**Ziisigobimizhiig**."

We are quiet, quiet as we climb the trail.
Quiet as mice and rabbits and deer.

We found a chipmunk and flowers,
pussy willows and geese.

But no moose.

"Maybe next time," says Grandpa.

"Next time," I say.
Next time we'll find moose.

"Mooz!"

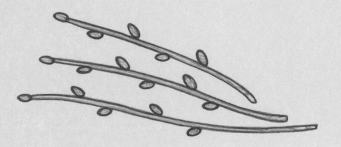

Grandpa introduces the forest plants and animals in English and Ojibwemowin.

Pussy willows: **Ziisigobimizhiig**
(ZEE-si-go-bi-mi-zheeg)

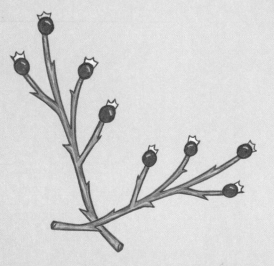

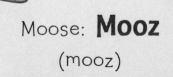

Moose: **Mooz**
(mooz)